THE BOXCAR CHILDREN
SURPRISE ISLAND
THE YELLOW HOUSE MYSTERY
MYSTERY RANCH
MIKE'S MYSTERY
BLUE BAY MYSTERY
THE WOODSHED MYSTERY
THE LIGHTHOUSE MYSTERY
MOUNTAIN TOP MYSTERY
SCHOOLHOUSE MYSTERY
CABOOSE MYSTERY
HOUSEBOAT MYSTERY
SNOWBOUND MYSTERY
TREE HOUSE MYSTERY
BICYCLE MYSTERY
MYSTERY IN THE SAND
MYSTERY BEHIND THE WALL
BUS STATION MYSTERY
BENNY UNCOVERS A MYSTERY
THE HAUNTED CABIN MYSTERY
THE DESERTED LIBRARY MYSTERY
THE ANIMAL SHELTER MYSTERY
THE OLD MOTEL MYSTERY
THE MYSTERY OF THE HIDDEN PAINTING
THE AMUSEMENT PARK MYSTERY
THE MYSTERY OF THE MIXED-UP ZOO
THE CAMP-OUT MYSTERY
THE MYSTERY GIRL
THE MYSTERY CRUISE
THE DISAPPEARING FRIEND MYSTERY
THE MYSTERY OF THE SINGING GHOST
THE MYSTERY IN THE SNOW
THE PIZZA MYSTERY
THE MYSTERY HORSE
THE MYSTERY AT THE DOG SHOW
THE CASTLE MYSTERY
THE MYSTERY OF THE LOST VILLAGE
THE MYSTERY ON THE ICE
THE MYSTERY OF THE PURPLE POOL
THE GHOST SHIP MYSTERY
THE MYSTERY IN WASHINGTON, DC
THE CANOE TRIP MYSTERY

THE MYSTERY OF THE HIDDEN BEACH
THE MYSTERY OF THE MISSING CAT
THE MYSTERY AT SNOWFLAKE INN
THE MYSTERY ON STAGE
THE DINOSAUR MYSTERY
THE MYSTERY OF THE STOLEN MUSIC
THE MYSTERY AT THE BALL PARK
THE CHOCOLATE SUNDAE MYSTERY
THE MYSTERY OF THE HOT AIR BALLOON
THE MYSTERY BOOKSTORE
THE PILGRIM VILLAGE MYSTERY
THE MYSTERY OF THE STOLEN BOXCAR
THE MYSTERY IN THE CAVE
THE MYSTERY ON THE TRAIN
THE MYSTERY AT THE FAIR
THE MYSTERY OF THE LOST MINE
THE GUIDE DOG MYSTERY
THE HURRICANE MYSTERY
THE PET SHOP MYSTERY
THE MYSTERY OF THE SECRET MESSAGE
THE FIREHOUSE MYSTERY
THE MYSTERY IN SAN FRANCISCO
THE NIAGARA FALLS MYSTERY
THE MYSTERY AT THE ALAMO
THE OUTER SPACE MYSTERY
THE SOCCER MYSTERY
THE MYSTERY IN THE OLD ATTIC
THE GROWLING BEAR MYSTERY
THE MYSTERY OF THE LAKE MONSTER
THE MYSTERY AT PEACOCK HALL
THE WINDY CITY MYSTERY
THE BLACK PEARL MYSTERY
THE CEREAL BOX MYSTERY
THE PANTHER MYSTERY
THE MYSTERY OF THE QUEEN'S JEWELS
THE STOLEN SWORD MYSTERY
THE BASKETBALL MYSTERY
THE MOVIE STAR MYSTERY
THE MYSTERY OF THE PIRATE'S MAP
THE GHOST TOWN MYSTERY
THE MYSTERY OF THE BLACK RAVEN
THE MYSTERY IN THE MALL

The Boxcar Children Mysteries

THE GHOST AT THE DRIVE-IN MOVIE

created by
GERTRUDE CHANDLER WARNER

Illustrated by Robert Papp

Albert Whitman & Company
Chicago, Illinois

Contents

THE GHOST AT THE DRIVE-IN MOVIE

CHAPTER 1

The Diamond in the Sky

Benny Alden was getting sleepy in the car. It was a long ride, and he had just closed his eyes. But then he heard his grandfather say something about . . . *a diamond!*

"Diamonds!" cried Benny. "Where?" The six-year-old loved mysteries and looking for hidden treasure.

His older sister Jessie looked back from the front seat of the minivan. "Oh, not real diamonds, Benny," she said, laughing.

Their grandfather nodded as he drove.

"I was just talking about the place where we're going," he said. "It's called the Diamond Drive-In Theater." The Aldens were on their way to visit a friend of Grandfather's, Frederick Fletcher, who lived in the countryside beyond Silver City.

"It's so great Mr. Fletcher owns a movie theater!" Violet said. At ten, she was the shyest of the Alden children, but even she couldn't hide her excitement.

Henry, who was the oldest, spoke up. "I've read about drive-in movie theaters, but I've never seen one. I guess they're pretty hard to find these days." He was fourteen and he liked looking up information on the internet.

"There used to be hundreds of them all over the country," said Grandfather. "There were dozens right here in Connecticut, back in the old days. Now there are only a few."

"I bet the front door of a drive-in theater has to be really wide," said Benny. "So that you can get your car inside."

Jessie had to keep from laughing again. "That's not how it works, Benny," she said.

Since she was twelve, she was always trying to explain things to her younger brother and sister. "Drive-in theaters are outdoors—right, Grandfather?"

"Indeed they are," said Grandfather.

"And then you sit in your car and watch the movie," Henry added. "So in a way, you're indoors, too—inside your car, at least."

"It sounds so strange," Violet said. "I can't wait to see what it's like."

"You'll see it soon," Grandfather said. They were driving past wide fields, and sometimes, shopping centers. "This used to be all farmland," he told the children, "But it's changing, bit by bit." There were lots of billboards and signs.

The minivan turned left. Jessie noticed a hot dog stand with a neon sign on one side of the road. On the other was a big store that sold new cars. She looked around for the drive-in theater.

"Look!" said Benny. "There's a great big billboard that's turned backwards!" He pointed out the window.

Grandfather grinned as he turned the car down a side road. They drove right past the thing that Benny was pointing at. "It's not a billboard," said Grandfather. "But can you guess what it is?"

Violet, who was an artist, had a good eye. "It's a movie screen!" she said. "See how it's all white on the other side?"

The screen stood with its back to the road. In front of it was a large gravel lot that stretched off towards the open field behind the theater.

"It looks like an empty parking lot," said Jessie.

"I think it *is* a parking lot," Henry said. "People must park their cars in rows—just like seats in a theater—and watch the movie."

Grandfather drove slowly around the edge of the big lot, towards a nearby house. He stopped the car, and he and the children got out. Their dog, Watch, woke up from his nap in the back seat. He leapt out happily and ran a circle around the car.

"I'm glad we brought Watch," Violet said.

"He'll have lots of space to run around."

Watch trotted over toward the house, which had a big front porch. A man had come outside to talk to Grandfather. He looked almost Grandfather's age, but he was shorter, and more stout.

"This is my good friend from college, Mr. Frederick Fletcher," Grandfather said.

"But everyone calls me Uncle Flick," the man added.

"Are you really everyone's uncle?" Benny asked.

Uncle Flick laughed. "No, not really," he said. "Though I do have a nephew. You'll meet him soon." When he laughed his face turned red, as if he had just been running. "And I got the nickname Uncle Flick because I own the Diamond Drive-In Theater—as you see, I live right next door to it! And I love to show 'flicks,' which is another word for—"

"Movies!" said Benny.

"Will we see one tonight?" Jessie asked.

"You'll see *two*," said Uncle Flick. "We

have double features every night starting just after sundown. Tonight we're showing *Island of the Horses* and *The Pirate Spy.*"

"*Pirate Spy?*" said Henry. "I can't wait!"

"Neither can I," said Violet. She'd been hoping to see *Island of the Horses* with Jessie at the Greenfield Mall.

"Now we just have to wait until the sun goes down," said Benny, looking up at the afternoon sky. "Hurry up, sun!"

By the time the Aldens had unpacked, the sun was much lower in the sky. The children stood on the porch of the Fletcher house and looked across at the drive-in theater. A few cars were already parked in the lot beneath the screen. The theater was now open for business!

"Flick's already at work," said Grandfather. "Let's find a spot to park the car and watch the movie. We can bring Watch with us."

They got back in the minivan and Grandfather drove slowly up and down the aisles of the car lot. Since it was still early there were plenty of spaces open. But the children wanted

to make sure they had a good view of the movie screen. Jessie felt the best spot would be in the front row. But Henry thought that was too close.

Violet giggled. "It's just like when we go to the movies at home!" she said.

They finally picked a spot near the middle of the fourth row. Grandfather parked the car right next to one of the odd-looking posts that stood alongside each parking space.

"What are those things for?" Jessie asked. There were metal boxes hanging on the posts. They looked like old-fashioned radios, and they were connected to the posts by long, thick cords.

"They're speakers from the old days," said Grandfather. "They're so you could hear the movie from inside the car." He rolled down the window. He took the speaker off the post and brought it inside. It had a special hook which he used to hang on the car door.

"Gosh," said Benny. "You mean you had to listen to the whole movie through that little box?"

"James Alden!" a voice called from outside. "You're not going to make your grandchildren listen to the whole movie through that old thing, are you?" Uncle Flick had driven up in a golf cart. He got out and walked over to Grandfather's window. "These days you can listen through your car stereo. You just tune in to a special station."

"Do the old speakers still work?" Henry asked.

"Sure! And some people still love using them. Don't know why, because they sound a bit crackly," Uncle Flick answered. "You'd really be roughing it."

"We've roughed it before!" said Benny. "When we lived in the boxcar."

After their parents died, Benny, Henry, Violet, and Jessie had run away instead of going to live with their grandfather. They had never met him, and they had heard he was mean, so they escaped to the woods. There they'd found an old boxcar, which they'd made their home. They found their dog, Watch, in the woods, too. When Grandfather found them at last they learned he wasn't mean at all, and they soon became a family again. As for the boxcar, Grandfather had it moved to the backyard of their home in Greenfield so they could use it as a clubhouse.

"I've heard you've had a lot of excitement in your lives already," Uncle Flick said. "I know a golf cart ride isn't terribly exciting, but would you like to take a tour? We have more than an hour before the movie starts."

Grandfather nodded at the children. "Go on. I'll stay here with Watch."

The children were getting seated in the golf cart when a young man approached. He wore a greasy apron tied around his waist and he slouched a little. He had brown hair that nearly covered his eyes. He half-smiled at them.

"Hey," he said. "You must be those kids from Greenfield. Hey. I'm Joey."

Uncle Flick scowled. "He means 'hello,' not 'hey,'" he told the Aldens. "Joey is my nephew. He lives nearby in Oakdale and he works here at the snack bar when he's home from college."

The children waved at Joey. "Hello," Henry said.

"Hey," said Joey. Then he turned around. "Gotta go back to work," he mumbled as he walked off. He seemed either unfriendly or shy. It was hard to tell which.

First Uncle Flick drove the golf cart over to the snack bar, where he brought out two bags of popcorn for the Aldens. They each told him thank-you as they took handfuls. The popcorn was hot and fresh and with just enough butter.

"You're welcome," he told the children. "We're proud of our popcorn here at the Diamond."

"What's that little building in front of the snack bar?" asked Violet as the golf cart started up again.

"That's the projection booth," said Uncle Flick. "That's where the film projector is."

Just then the door to the booth opened and a young woman stepped out. She looked to be the same age as Joey Fletcher. She had short, boyish dark hair. She looked surprised when she saw Uncle Flick and the Aldens, as if she had been caught doing something she shouldn't. But then she smiled and waved.

"That's Amy Castella. She runs the film projector," said Uncle Flick. "Where are you going, Amy?" he called.

"Oh, me?" said Amy, a bit nervously. "I wasn't going anywhere. Just getting the movie ready! That's all!" She waved again and went back inside the booth.

"She's always very busy before the show," Uncle Flick told the children. "Maybe you'll meet her later. Let's see how the crowd is doing." He steered the golf cart down another aisle.

There were dozens of vehicles now—cars and minivans and wagons, and lots of families. Some people stayed in their cars, but many were sitting in lawn chairs that they'd brought and set up in front of their cars. They had radios so they could hear the movie. Everyone was enjoying the last bit of daylight on this late summer evening, and Uncle Flick waved hello to several families.

"It feels like Greenfield Park before the Fourth of July fireworks," Henry said.

"There are even dogs here!" Benny said as they passed a minivan where a happy-looking beagle leaned its head out the window.

"Yes, we allow them here, as long as they're well-behaved and don't run free," said Uncle Flick.

"That's so great," said Jessie, who loved dogs. "You can't watch a movie with your dog at a regular theater."

"Wow," Violet said suddenly, "Look at that car!"

They saw a large red car decorated with blue and white balloons. The car was shiny and looked brand new. There was a sign on the hood that said BRING YOURSELF TO BRINKER'S AUTO! In front of the car was a man in a suit jacket the same color as the car. He smiled a very big smile when he saw the golf cart and its passengers.

"Kids, this is Dan Brinker," said Uncle Flick. "He sells cars and his business is right across the road from here. Dan, this is Jessie,

Henry, Benny, and Violet Alden—they're here visiting from Greenfield with their grandfather."

"Pleased to meet you," said Dan. "I just love coming here and meeting new people and showing off the latest deals at Brinker's Auto. Because what's a better place for car lovers than a drive-in movie theater? I love cars, too. And I love this theater. I love popcorn!"

"So do we!" said Benny. "Want some?" He held out one of the bags of popcorn.

"Why, thank you," Dan said. He reached out and took a big handful. "Thank you very much." He took another handful, and then another.

"Dan comes here three times a week to show off the cars he's selling," Uncle Flick explained. "He has a different car every time. And he likes to hand out all kinds of goodies for free."

"Have a bucket!" Dan said. He handed each of them a bright blue plastic bucket with the words GET SPEEDY DEALS AT BRINKER'S AUTO printed on it. "It's just so you'll remember when you buy a car at Brinker's Auto, you get speedy service!"

"Thanks," said Jessie, who was a bit puzzled. "We can always use . . . buckets."

"Everyone loves buckets!" said Dan. They all had to laugh at this. Dan laughed, too.

"That Dan Brinker is quite a character," said Uncle Flick as the golf cart went down the aisle. "He's always clowning around. I suppose it helps him sell cars. And he might—oh, excuse me for a minute." The walkie-talkie on his belt was beeping. "I have to answer this." He picked up the walkie-talkie and pushed a button. "What is it, Nora?"

Benny tried to hear the voice on the walkie-talkie, but it was too scratchy.

"Something's wrong," Uncle Flick told the Aldens. "There's a problem at the front gate." He sounded almost angry.

Jessie's eyes grew wide as she looked around at her sister and brothers. "What's going on?" she asked.

"We'll have to head right over," said Uncle Flick, as he turned the golf cart around.

"It sounds like trouble," said Henry.

"It sure is," replied Uncle Flick.

CHAPTER 2

The Sound of Trouble

The ticket booth was at the front gate of the theater. When Uncle Flick and the Aldens arrived, they saw that the woman who worked there was arguing with a couple in a white Jeep. The couple was very upset.

"What's the problem here?" Uncle Flick asked as he got out of the golf cart.

The man in the Jeep pointed to the ticket seller. "She won't let us in to see the movie. All because of some silly business about hot dogs!"

"I'm just doing my job," said the ticket seller. "And you can't bring in food from Duke's Dogs. That's the rule!" She tapped a sign on the window that said FOOD FROM DUKE'S NOT ALLOWED AT THE DIAMOND DRIVE-IN THEATER.

The woman in the Jeep waved a red-and-white striped paper bag, and Benny could smell french fries. She said, "I don't understand. This hot dog stand is right next door! We didn't know until we got here that we couldn't bring in the food we'd bought."

Jessie thought the woman had a point.

"Flick Fletcher!" shouted a furious voice from behind them. They all turned and saw a thin older man in a red-and-white striped shirt marching towards them. "Are you giving my customers trouble?"

"They're my customers, too, Duke," said Uncle Flick. He glared at the man.

"I think that man owns the hot dog stand next door," Henry whispered to Jessie. "His name must be Mr. Duke."

"I know why you made that ridiculous rule,

Flick," said Mr. Duke. "You're trying to get back at me . . . for building my sign too close your precious screen."

Now that it was getting dark, the neon sign for Duke's Dogs was shining brightly. The children had noticed it earlier from their spot in the theater—it could be seen beyond the movie screen.

"It IS too close!" said Uncle Flick. "And too bright! But a rule is a rule. We sell food here already!"

Mr. Duke had a mean smile. "*Your* food isn't as good," he said. "If it weren't for that rule, Duke's Dogs would put your little snack bar out of business!"

Uncle Flick's face got very red. "Why . . . you . . ." he began to say.

Violet had been looking at the Jeep and she noticed something. She leaned over and whispered to Henry.

"Excuse me," Henry called out. He got out of the golf cart. "My sister noticed the license plate on the Jeep is from New York. Are you from out of town?" he asked the couple.

"Why, yes," said the woman. "We're here on vacation."

Jessie stood up, too. "Uncle Flick, these people didn't know about the rule. They've never been here before."

Uncle Flick looked down at his feet. "Yes, you're right," he said. "They couldn't have known."

"We'll be sure not to break the rule next time," the man in the Jeep said.

"You can go on in," Uncle Flick told the couple. "I'm very sorry about the trouble. Enjoy the show."

"And enjoy the hot dogs, too," said Mr. Duke. Uncle Flick shot him an angry look.

The white Jeep drove through the gate into the theater. The children were glad to see the problem was resolved.

"I'm glad they got to keep the hot dogs, too," Benny whispered to Jessie. "They sure smell good."

"Thank you for speaking up, kids," Uncle Flick told the Aldens. "Sometimes it helps to have another point of view."

Mr. Duke spoke up then. "Well, if you want *my* point of view," he said, "one of these days, Flick, that temper of yours will get you in trouble, and you won't be able to talk your way out of it." He turned around and walked back to his hot dog stand.

Uncle Flick shook his head as he drove the golf cart back into the drive-in. "Mr. Duke and I used to be friends. But we haven't gotten along in years," he said sadly.

Jessie couldn't stop thinking of what Mr. Duke had said. What did he mean by *trouble?* It sounded almost like a threat.

*   *   *

The children returned to the minivan. Grandfather had brought back dinner from the snack bar. There were slices of pizza, chicken fingers, and bowls of chili.

"Good thing we didn't fill up on popcorn," said Jessie, as she took a pizza slice.

"I never fill up on anything!" said Benny. It was true that the youngest Alden always had a great appetite.

"This chicken is delicious," Violet said. "Mr. Duke was wrong when he said that the food at the Diamond Drive-In isn't as good."

"It's great," said Henry. "But there aren't hot dogs here. And I could see how someone might want a hot dog at the movies."

Everyone agreed it was too bad that Uncle Flick and Mr. Duke didn't get along with each other.

The sky over the drive-in theater had darkened to deep blue, and a few stars had come out.

"Look at the screen!" said Benny. "Here comes the movie!"

They turned the car radio on so they could hear the movie. Violet and Benny moved up to the front seat with Jessie so they could have a good view out the windshield. Henry and Grandfather sat in the back seat, since they were the tallest. Watch curled up in Jessie's lap.

First they watched trailers for upcoming movies, and then a funny commercial for Brinker's Auto showing Dan Brinker on roller skates. "I love speedy deals!" he shouted.

Finally, it was time for the movie *Island of the Horses* to begin. The Aldens fell quiet as they followed the story, which was about a boy who had been in a shipwreck and was on a raft looking for land. It was so good that they began to forget they were even in the car. Jessie felt like she was in the scene, too, out on the softly rolling sea—

"One-two-three o'clock, four o'clock rock! Five, six, seven o'clock, eight o'clock rock—" The sudden loud music from the radio surprised everyone.

"Yikes! What's that?" Jessie cried. "Did someone change the station?"

"It just changed by itself! And it's really loud!" shouted Benny.

The music blasting out of the radio was clearly not the sound that was supposed to go with the movie. Henry looked around at the other cars. People reached for their radio dials or covered their ears.

"Oh, no!" Violet said. "It's ruining the movie!"

The children got out of the car and started running towards the projection booth. Car horns were honking. "Fix the sound!" someone yelled. When they got to the projection booth they saw the door was wide open.

"No one's there!" Jessie said, gasping. But then they saw Amy Castella running towards the booth. She hurried up the steps in a panic. Henry and Jessie could see her fumbling with the controls inside the booth. Finally, the cars stopped honking.

"That was strange," said Henry.

Violet ran up behind them. "It's fixed now. You can hear the movie again."

They went back to the car and watched the rest of the movie. The children had a feeling this wouldn't be the last strange thing to happen.

After the movie ended, the children lined up at the snack bar to get ice cream. They were standing near a door marked OFFICE when suddenly it opened and Uncle Flick and Amy came out.

"I just don't know what happened!" Amy

was telling Uncle Flick. "The sound just accidentally switched, I guess!"

"Why weren't you in the booth?" Uncle Flick asked her. "You're not supposed to go anywhere, not with all these pranks that have been happening lately. Where were you?"

"I just stepped out for a second!" Amy cried. "I promise I'll keep a better eye on things!" She hurried off back to her booth. And Uncle Flick walked back into his office, shaking his head.

The children looked at each other. What were all these other pranks about? Why were they happening?

* * *

"Maybe two movies in a row is a little too much for Benny," Jessie said later on, as they all trudged up the front steps of the Fletcher house. Grandfather carried Benny, who had fallen asleep not too long after the start of the second movie.

"He'll get another chance to see *Pirate*

Spy," Henry said. "It's showing tomorrow night, too."

Benny woke up just then. "I like pirates," he said. Then he yawned a very big yawn.

After the children got ready for bed in their guest room, they came back downstairs to say good-night to Grandfather. He was in the kitchen drinking coffee with Uncle Flick.

"I'm so glad you kids could come visit the Diamond Drive-In," Uncle Flick told the Aldens. "At least while I'm still running it."

"What do you mean?" Violet asked. "Is it going to close down?" The thought made her sad. She knew there weren't many drive-in theaters anymore.

"No, I hope not," Uncle Flick replied. "But I was just telling your grandfather— I think I'm going to sell the place."

"Is it because of all the pranks?" Jessie asked.

"Oh, you've heard about those, have you?" Uncle Flick said. "Yes, we've had a few lately. Someone fiddled with the lens on the projector to make the movie blurry. Someone poured popcorn salt into the soda fountain. That's been a pain! But the main reason for selling the place is just . . . well, my job isn't as much fun anymore."

"Don't you like showing movies?" asked Violet.

"Yes I do," said Uncle Flick. "But I used to do more than show movies. We'd have fireworks after the show, and contests, and Kids' Night. Things like that were always good for business. And they were fun. But they're a lot of work, too. I'm getting older and don't have as much pep. I'm feeling more and more like this tired and tuckered-out fellow here." He smiled at Benny.

"I'm not tired," Benny said. "Or tuckered out." He yawned again. Everyone laughed.

"But don't worry," Uncle Flick went on. "I won't sell the theater to just anyone. I'm going to make sure that whoever buys this place keeps it open. They'll have to promise me that movie screen will always stay standing."

Jessie thought of something. "What about your nephew Joey? Maybe one day he'll want to run the theater."

Uncle Flick sighed. "I doubt it. All he wants to do is leave this town and—"

Screech!

Suddenly outside there was the sound of tires squealing, and then a *thud*. Watch, who had been napping near the front door, leapt up and started barking.

"What on Earth was that?" Uncle Flick said. He and the Aldens hurried out to the porch.

"It's Dan Brinker's car!" said Henry. "Or at least, the one he's trying to sell."

The shiny red car had driven off the road. Now it was in a small ditch. Some of the balloons that had decorated the car had come loose. The car door was open. Dan Brinker was hurrying about trying to pick up the balloons. He looked pale and shaken.

"Are you all right, Mr. Brinker?" Henry asked.

"What happened, Dan?" Uncle Flick called out.

"It was . . . it was a ghost!" Dan Brinker said, gasping. "I saw it. Over there." He pointed towards the darkness of the outdoor theater.

"A ghost?" Benny whispered. "Wow."

"I . . . I was taking the back road. I was driving back to my office," Dan went on. "And then I saw the ghost! It was walking along! And . . . I suppose I began to panic . . . and I lost control of the car . . ." He took several deep breaths and wiped his brow with his handkerchief.

"Do you think it was really a ghost?" Jessie asked Henry quietly.

"No, of course not," said Henry. But he wasn't so sure himself.

"This ghost stuff is nonsense, Dan," Uncle Flick said. "You must have been seeing things! Maybe it was one of those balloons. It's foolish to try to drive with those all over your car."

"I know what I saw, Flick," said Dan. "And what I saw was a ghost!" He straightened up and smoothed his hair. "Now, if you don't mind, I'll be on my way. Thank goodness the car wasn't hurt. I'm just . . . spooked, that's all."

He got back into the car and closed the

door. He started the car and drove off.

"I wonder what that was all about," said Grandfather.

"He sure looked like he'd seen a ghost," said Henry. Everyone agreed.

"Wait—what's that?" Violet asked.

Just then, they all heard footsteps coming out of the darkness behind the road. Benny held his breath. *Was it the ghost?*

But it was only Joey Fletcher. "What was all that racket?" he asked his uncle.

"Nothing," said Uncle Flick. "I thought you'd finished cleaning up the snack bar an hour ago. What took you so long?"

"Oh . . . I was just being extra careful. I wanted to make sure nobody was trying to make any more trouble," Joey said. He shrugged and went inside the house.

By now it was past bedtime. Jessie and her brothers and sister went back upstairs. They all sat on the big bed Jessie and Violet were sharing and looked out the window towards the dark drive-in theater. They could see the screen in the moonlight.

"There really is a lot of trouble here," Jessie remarked.

"Yes," said Violet. "So many strange things are happening."

"I think it *is* haunted!" Benny said. "And I want to see the ghost."

"Benny, you know there's no such thing as ghosts," Henry said. "Now let's go to bed."

Jessie added, "Yes, Mr. Brinker was just seeing things that weren't really there."

"Maybe you're right," Benny said. But he also thought to himself: *Maybe not.*

CHAPTER 3

Strange Intermission

"Uncle Flick, is there anything we can do to help out while we're here?" Henry asked. "Besides fixing breakfast, I mean."

They were eating breakfast with Uncle Flick in the kitchen of the Fletcher house. Grandfather had brought back muffins from a bakery in town, and the children had helped wash and cut fresh fruit.

"Yes, we can lend a hand around the theater," Jessie added.

It was true—the Aldens always liked being

helpful. But they also hoped that by helping out around the theater, they could figure out why so many odd things were happening.

"Why, thank you," said Uncle Flick. "There are plenty of things you can do before the theater opens tonight. Pick up litter, check to make sure the car speakers are working, stuff like that."

"I can test popcorn!" Benny said. "I can taste it to make sure there's enough butter!"

Uncle Flick laughed at this. "No need to do that, Benny! But we'll figure out a job for you."

After lunch, the children got right to work. Henry carefully checked the cords on all the speakers. Jessie and Violet picked up litter with special spiked poles. And Benny's job was to bring everyone water and supplies. Uncle Flick found Joey's old dirt bike for Benny to ride. They filled the front basket with water bottles and trash bags.

"You can ride over to the projection booth and see if Amy needs anything," said Uncle Flick.

"I'll head right over!" said Benny. He pedaled off across the lot.

But when he got to the booth, Amy wasn't there. So he got back on the bike to find Jessie and Violet.

Meanwhile, Henry had finished checking the speakers. He went to the snack bar to ask Joey if he needed any help. When he walked inside the lights were on, but the place was empty.

"Hello?" he called. But there was no answer.

Jessie and Violet had picked up all the litter they could find on the lot. They had nearly filled a whole bag of garbage.

"I'm getting thirsty," Violet said. "I think I saw Benny riding his bike over by the snack bar. I'll go find him and get some water for us."

"Good idea," said Jessie. "It's getting hot out!"

Violet walked off across the lot. Jessie looked up at the movie screen, which was shining brightly in the sun. She realized there would be shade on the other side of the screen, so she walked behind it.

It was nice and cool behind the screen. Jessie picked up a few pieces of litter and looked around. She noticed a large bundle near the back of the screen—it was something rolled up, like a tent. She would be sure to ask Uncle Flick what it was. Just then, she heard Henry calling her name, and she went out to the front of the theater.

"Have you seen Joey?" Henry asked. "He was supposed to be at the snack bar, but he's not there."

"No," Jessie said. "What about Benny? Violet's looking for him. He's got the water, and we're thirsty!"

"So am I," said Henry. He turned and looked around the lot. "Look, there he is now!"

They both saw Benny riding his bike near the front gate.

"Benny! Over here!" Jessie called. But Benny wasn't paying attention. He liked the bike very much.

Henry groaned. "We'll have to go over there to get our water," he said. So he and Jessie ran across the lot to Benny.

Over on the other side of the theater, Violet hadn't seen Benny at all. She was still looking for him by the snack bar. She was walking along the edge of the building when she heard a voice around the corner. "Benny?" she said.

But it wasn't Benny. Amy and Joey were there, and they had been talking. They both jumped a little when they saw Violet. Violet jumped, too.

"Gosh! I didn't mean to surprise you," said Violet.

Joey stood up straighter and pushed the hair out of his eyes. "Uh, what do you mean, 'surprise?'"

"Oh . . . well . . . I thought I interrupted you while you were talking," Violet replied.

"We weren't talking!" said Amy. "I mean, we weren't talking about anything important."

"Like, why would we be?" said Joey.

Violet thought they were acting oddly. "I'm sorry. Never mind," she said. She was turning to leave when suddenly Amy said, "Wait!" and ran up to Violet.

"What is it?" Violet asked.

Amy's voice was sharp. "Do you see that storage shed over there?" she asked. She pointed to a long low building on the far edge of the theater grounds.

"Y-yes," said Violet.

"You and your sister and brothers need to stay away from there. If any of you go in there you'll . . . you'll be in trouble. Do you understand?" Amy sounded very serious.

Violet nodded.

"You be sure to tell them," said Amy. She marched off towards the projection booth. Joey went back inside the snack bar. And Violet took a deep breath. She was glad to see Jessie and Henry walking back across the lot.

"What was that all about?" Jessie asked her.

Violet told her sister and Henry what had just happened.

"There's something strange about Amy," Jessie remarked. "She always acts like we've caught her at something."

"Well, she's never where she's supposed to be," Violet said. "Come to think of it, neither is Joey."

"*And neither is Benny!*" said Henry, looking around. "Did he ride off on his bike again?"

Benny had indeed ridden off again. After he'd given Henry and Jessie their water bottles he'd decided to find Violet, too. He wondered if she was on the other side of the theater, so he rode along the edge of the lot until he saw something he hadn't noticed before. It was an old storage shed. Benny got off his bike and walked up to the open door to peek inside.

What he saw inside made his eyes widen. He couldn't believe what he saw. "I have to tell Henry and Jessie and Violet about this!" he whispered.

He ran back to his bike and rode off across the theater lot. Soon he saw Jessie running up to him.

"There you are!" said Jessie. "You shouldn't ride off like that without telling anyone where you're going," she said firmly. Jessie often acted like a mother to Benny.

"I'm sorry," Benny said.

"It's important," she added. "Because there are places where you're not supposed to go. Like the storage shed. Amy told Violet that if any of us go in there we'll all be in trouble. Okay?"

"O-okay," said Benny. He did not want anyone to be in trouble. So he did not tell Jessie that he'd been to the shed. He would not tell anyone what he'd seen inside.

*   *   *

Evening came, and the drive-in theater opened for the night.

"Are you sure you don't mind seeing *Island of the Horses* and *Pirate Spy* again?" Grandfather asked the children.

"We don't mind," said Jessie. Sometimes the children liked watching the same movie more than once. But they also wanted to find out more about the pranks at the drive-in—and the ghost, too.

"Let's find a spot for the car," Grandfather said. "And then I'll walk back over to the Fletcher house and read my book on the porch. You can call me on my cell phone if you need anything."

Soon the minivan was in a good spot in the third row of the drive-in. It was still twilight, and the Alden children decided to walk around to look for anything unusual. Henry walked with Violet and Benny. They saw Dan Brinker in the second row. Tonight he had a shiny silver car decorated with green and blue balloons.

"Maybe he can tell us more about the ghost," Violet replied.

"Let's talk to him at intermission," Henry said.

"What's in-ter-mish-un?" Benny asked.

"That's the break in the middle of a show," Henry said. "Here at the theater, it's the break between the first movie and the second one."

Meanwhile, Jessie was walking Watch. They were near the projection booth when she heard a voice call, "Jessie?"

It was Amy Castella. She was standing in the doorway of the booth. "Hi. Er . . . could you do me a favor?" Amy asked. "Could you just keep an eye on the booth while I run and get a soda?"

Jessie didn't know what to say for a moment. Amy hadn't been very friendly.

"Listen," Amy went on. "I'm sorry about today. I guess I wasn't very nice to your sister. It's just that things have been crazy around here lately."

"What happened with the sound last night?" Jessie asked.

Amy looked sheepish. "I wish I knew," she said. "But I know it wasn't an accident. There's no way the sound could have just switched like that! I need to be truthful with Uncle Flick and tell him . . ."

"Tell him what?" asked Jessie.

"That someone must have played a trick last night. Someone was in the booth when I was out."

"Oh, no," said Jessie.

"So will you please stay here for a moment while I get a soda?" Amy begged.

Jessie nodded.

"Thank you so much. I'll be right back!" Amy ran off towards the snack bar.

Jessie sat on the front steps of the booth with Watch. "Amy's being friendlier," she told Watch. "But why does it seem like she's still hiding something?"

After Amy returned to the booth, Jessie and Watch went back to the minivan. As the first movie began, Jessie told Henry, Violet, and Benny what had happened.

"Perhaps Amy is behind the pranks," said Henry. "After all, she lied to Uncle Flick yesterday. She said the sound problem was an accident when it wasn't."

"Or maybe she feels guilty about leaving the booth," Violet said.

"Both she and Joey keep sneaking off for some reason," Jessie pointed out.

"And what about the ghost?" Benny asked.

"Benny, there's no such thing as ghosts," Henry reminded him. "But . . . maybe someone is trying to make the place look haunted."

"They are!" Benny said. "I mean, maybe whoever is doing the pranks is making the ghost, too."

"That's true," said Jessie. "When the movie is over, let's find Dan Brinker and ask him about the ghost."

Violet started giggling. "Oh my gosh! I almost forgot we were watching a movie! With people all around!"

Henry laughed, too. "But since we're in a car, nobody else can hear us. So nobody is saying 'sshhhhh!'"

"Drive-in movies are the best kind!" said Benny.

An hour later, *Island of the Horses* had ended. Jessie and Violet thought it was even better the second time around. As soon as the lights came up over the theater lot, they set out towards Dan Brinker's car to talk to him about the "ghost" he had seen the night before.

The balloon-covered car was still in the second row. But Dan wasn't there.

"Maybe he went to the snack bar," said Jessie. "Let's go see if he's waiting in line."

As the children walked towards the snack bar they heard a funny sound behind them. *Zzzzt-zzzzt-zzzzt!* It sounded like a bug zapper. *Zzzzt! Zzzzzzzt!* Watch heard it, too, and started barking.

Everyone in the theater was looking and pointing towards something in the sky near the screen. The children turned around and saw what it was. It was the neon sign for Duke's Dogs. Something was very wrong with it. *Zzzz, zzzt,* it went, as it flickered and sputtered.

And then it went dark!

CHAPTER 4

Bad Sign

"What just happened to the Duke's Dogs sign?" Jessie said.

"I don't know," said Henry. "But I'm sure Mr. Duke isn't happy."

"Look, there he is now," said Violet. "He just walked through the front gate."

Mr. Duke wasn't just unhappy—he was angry. The children watched as he marched up the center aisle of the drive-in theater. "Flick!" he yelled. "What's all this about?"

Uncle Flick came out of his office scratching

his head. "What's all what about?" he replied.

"My sign!" barked Mr. Duke. "I know you always hated that sign. So you cut the power to it, didn't you? You broke it!"

"I did not!" Uncle Flick said sharply. "I've been here in the office all along!"

"Then maybe that nephew of yours did it," Duke said. "I've seen him sneaking around the theater after hours!"

"Joey has every right to be on my property," Uncle Flick growled.

"But not on mine! I promise I'll get to the bottom of this!" Mr. Duke shouted. He turned around and marched back towards his hot dog stand.

"Can you believe that?" Jessie said. "Mr. Duke thinks someone here broke the sign!"

"Maybe it was just an accident," said Violet. But even she didn't think it could be an accident. None of the Aldens did. Suddenly they heard a voice behind them.

"What happened?" It was Joey Fletcher.

"Weren't you just at work at the snack bar?" Henry asked him.

"Nah, I was on break," Joey said. He shuffled past them and walked back towards the snack bar.

The Aldens all looked at each other. They were all thinking the same thing: if Joey wasn't at his job when the sign went dark, then where was he?

The children waited until the second movie was over. The moment the lights came back up, they ran over to Dan Brinker's car. This time he was there. He waved and got out of the car to talk to them.

"Hello, kids!" Dan said. "Did you like *Pirate Spy?*"

"We sure did," said Benny. "My favorite part was when the captain found the buried treasure chest."

"And he found the gold coins!" said Dan. "I loved that part! I love movies! It's been quite a night!"

"Actually," Henry said. "We want to hear about last night. And the ghost."

Dan Brinker's face went pale.

"There have been a lot of pranks here at

the theater lately," Jessie said. "Do you think the ghost could have been another trick?"

"You mean . . . someone wants to make the theater seem haunted?" said Dan Brinker. "Why . . . yes. Why didn't I think of that?"

"We're just trying to figure out who is causing problems at the theater," said Jessie.

"We solve mysteries," said Benny. "And we're good at them!"

"Well, if you ask me," Dan said in a low voice, "I think that Mr. Duke is up to no good. Maybe *he's* causing all the trouble. He sure doesn't like Uncle Flick."

"Thank you," said Jessie. She was writing things down in her notebook. "That's very helpful."

"Would you like some popcorn, Mr. Brinker?" Benny asked. He held out his bag. He remembered how much the car salesman had liked popcorn the night before.

"I would love some—" Dan said. He started to reach for the bag but stopped himself. "—but I'd better not." He kept his hands in his pockets.

Benny wondered why a man who loved

popcorn as much as he did could turn it down. Jessie saw, and wondered, too.

"Maybe his hands are just dirty," she explained to Benny, as they walked back to their car.

"Bye, kids!" Dan Brinker called after them. "Good luck solving the mystery."

* * *

There was plenty for the children to talk about at bedtime.

"Do you think what Dan Brinker said about Mr. Duke is true?" Violet asked her sister and brothers. "Do you think he's causing the problems?"

"I don't know," said Henry. "The problem that happened tonight was with his sign. Whoever was playing a prank played it on him."

"There are so many things going on right now!" Jessie said. "Uncle Flick and Mr. Duke don't like each other. Amy and Joey are always in the wrong places at the wrong times. And then we have to figure out where this ghost is coming from."

"I think the ghost comes from the haunted house," Benny said.

"What on earth are you talking about, Benny?" Violet said. "What haunted house?"

"I mean, *a* haunted house," Benny replied. "Just a haunted house somewhere. Because that's where ghosts live." He wanted to tell them about something he'd seen in the storage shed. But he knew he couldn't, since he wasn't supposed to look in the shed in the first place.

"Benny, what have we told you about ghosts?" Henry said. "There's no such thing. Right, Jessie?"

But Jessie wasn't listening. She was looking at something out the window of their guest room. Her eyes were getting wider and wider.

"There's . . . there's something out there," she said. "Something walking around."

"What?" cried Violet. "Where?" She rushed to the window where Jessie was seated. There was another window next to it and Henry and Benny pressed their faces against the glass to peer out.

"It's over by the fence next to the screen," said Jessie. "Do you see it?"

The other three Aldens looked where Jessie had told them. They all saw an eerie figure all in white walking along the fence. The figure seemed to walk and float at the same time.

"It's the ghost!" Benny said, amazed.

"What should we do?" Violet asked.

"Let's tell Uncle Flick!" Jessie said.

A few moments later they were all hurrying down the front steps of the Fletcher house. They ran across the lot towards the front of the theater.

"Wait a minute," Uncle Flick called. He went to the side of the house and opened a metal box that hung on the wall. He flipped some switches. The lights over the theater lot came on.

The children stopped running and looked around under the bright light. Uncle Flick and Grandfather joined them. Watch ran up,

too, and barked at all the excitement.

"The person I saw was right over here," said Jessie, pointing to the fence near the screen. "I couldn't tell if it was a man or a woman."

"I saw the person, too," said Henry. "But as soon as the lights came on, he—or she—disappeared!"

"I know it's not a ghost," said Violet. "But it sure looked like one."

Uncle Flick nodded. "There's definitely something strange happening around here. Your grandfather tells me you children solve mysteries, is that right?"

"Yes, sir," Henry replied. "And we'd like to look around and see if there's any sign of the person who was just here."

"In the morning, that is," said Jessie. "It's much too late at night now." The children looked up at the moon. Even though it was not a cold night, they all felt a little bit of a chill.

The next day, the children searched all around the corner of the theater lot where they had seen the ghostly figure. Henry had hoped there would be footprints, but the ground was too dusty and dry.

"At least there's no litter on the ground either," Violet said. "Jessie and I did a good job yesterday."

This made Jessie remember something else.

"You know, I saw something odd over behind the screen yesterday. Some kind of bundle."

"A ghost costume?" Benny said.

"Actually, I don't know what it was," Jessie said. "I meant to ask Uncle Flick about it." She walked around the screen and went behind it. The other children followed. "Whatever it was, it's gone now," said Jessie.

"We should still look around here anyway," said Henry.

"It's boring back here," said Benny. He had gone over to one of the two rusty metal ladders that went up the back of the screen. He grabbed one of the rungs and began to play like a monkey.

Jessie frowned. "Benny, that ladder's not a jungle gym. Come help us search the ground for clues instead."

"Aw, okay," Benny muttered. He let go of

the ladder. He sat down and found an old white balloon scrap and played with that instead. He stretched and pulled it.

"Hey, look," Violet pointed out. "There are car tire tracks back here. But there's no road or driveway."

"That's interesting," said Henry. "But there wasn't a car back here last night. Look where it was parked. If it were here last night, we would have seen it when Uncle Flick turned the lights on."

"I guess you're right," Violet said with a sigh. "I wonder why someone would park a car back here, though."

"Whatever the reason," Jessie said, "It probably has nothing to do with the ghost."

She shook her head sadly. The others knew how she felt. Sometimes, mysteries about ghosts were the hardest mysteries to solve.

CHAPTER 5

A Popping Good Idea

The children hadn't had any luck finding clues at the theater that morning. They were glad when Uncle Flick and Grandfather offered to take them out to lunch in Oakdale. The Aldens knew they needed a break.

On their way into town the children watched the signs and billboards along the way.

"Wow," said Jessie. "I've counted three billboards for Dan Brinker's Auto Emporium!"

As they drove into town, they could see

even more ads for Dan's business. One was painted on the side of a building. There was even a sidewalk bench painted with the words WHY WAIT? GET SPEEDY DEALS AT BRINKER'S AUTO.

"He's everywhere!" Henry said, laughing.

"He certainly is," said Uncle Flick. "He'd put an ad up on the water tower in the middle of town if he could!"

Grandfather found a parking spot in front of a family restaurant.

"I can't wait to have lunch!" Benny said as they walked up to the door of the restaurant.

"You'll have to wash your hands first," said Henry. "What on Earth did you get on them?"

Benny looked down at his palms, which were covered with gritty red-brown dust. "I don't know!" he said.

Jessie took Benny's hand and looked closer. "It looks like rust. I bet you got it when you were playing on that old metal ladder behind the movie screen."

"Oops," said Benny. "I'll wash up!"

At the restaurant table a few minutes later, Jessie smiled as Benny reached for a basket of rolls with clean hands. It reminded her of something she'd noticed the day before, but she couldn't remember what.

The waiter brought out bowls of macaroni and cheese, bacon-lettuce-and-tomato sandwiches, and salads with big croutons. Everything was so good, they forgot about the strange things that had been happening at the drive-in theater. It wasn't until lunch was nearly over that Uncle Flick even mentioned the theater at all.

"I've got some news to share," he said. He put down his napkin. "This afternoon I'm visiting the bank. I'm going to talk to my banker about selling the Diamond Drive-In."

Benny stopped with his fork in the air. Violet, Jessie, and Henry fell silent, too.

"Is there someone who wants to buy it, Flick?" Grandfather asked.

"As a matter of fact, there is," Uncle Flick answered. "Dan Brinker."

Grandfather raised an eyebrow. "That car

salesman? *He* wants to run the movie theater?"

"That's what he told the banker," said Uncle Flick.

"He told us he loves movies!" Benny said.

Uncle Flick nodded. "I know it seems a bit odd that Dan would want to run the theater. But he seems to love the place. And he's a good businessman, too. I trust him."

"Yes, but—" Jessie spoke up. "What about Joey? Couldn't he run the theater? He's almost old enough."

Uncle Flick looked thoughtful. "I would be so happy if Joey took over the business. But I don't think he wants to. He works hard, but he's always disappearing on the job. I think it means he doesn't want to be there. But Dan, on the other hand—he comes to the theater because he likes it. Of course, I haven't made my final decision. That will take time. This is only the first meeting with my banker."

"It's a big decision," Grandfather said.

The children agreed.

* * *

While Uncle Flick met with the banker, the Aldens went shopping along the main street of the little town. Then they all drove back to the drive-in theater in the afternoon.

As the minivan drove up along the road at the edge of the theater, they saw something was very wrong. There was a police car parked by the snack bar! Grandfather drove straight across the lot to the little building.

Joey and Amy were standing near the police car taking with the policewoman. Uncle Flick rushed over to join them. The Aldens could see that Joey looked very upset.

"There's been another prank! It's the worst yet," he cried.

The Aldens, Uncle Flick, Joey, and Amy walked with the police officer around the kitchen of the snack bar. It was a mess! The refrigerators had been unplugged and left open for hours, and the food inside was spoiled. Someone had dumped oil all over the popcorn bags and ruined them. Worst of all, the cord to the popcorn machine had been cut.

"Joey! Why weren't you keeping an eye on things?" Uncle Flick shouted.

"Now, Mr. Fletcher," the policewoman said. "Your nephew tells me he came in here at the same time he always does, and he found it this way. Whoever did this broke in here hours ago."

"They must have done it when we left to go to lunch," Jessie said.

"Sometimes I come in here early," Joey said. "I wish I'd done that today! Maybe if I had, I could've stopped the person who did this! But I was off working on . . . something else. I wish I'd been here earlier!"

The children saw that Joey felt just awful. Maybe he really did care about the movie theater, more than Uncle Flick realized.

"It's all right," Uncle Flick told Joey, patting him on the shoulder. "We never thought someone would do something like this."

"But what do we do now?" asked Amy. "The theater opens in less than two hours.

The popcorn machine is broken, and we won't have any food to sell!"

Jessie opened a cabinet door under the counter. Inside was a big bin full of popcorn kernels. "Uncle Flick," she asked. "Can this popcorn be popped on the stove?"

"Sure it can," said Uncle Flick. "Popcorn's popcorn!"

Jessie looked around at her brothers and sisters and said, "We've got an idea."

A few minutes later, the Aldens, Uncle Flick, and Joey were in the kitchen at the Fletcher house. They had brought the popcorn and a bottle of oil. They searched the kitchen cabinets and found two very big pots. Henry measured the oil and soon one of the big pots was heating up the kernels. It wasn't long before they heard the first pop! The pops came faster and faster. *Pop! Pop! Pop-pop-pop-pop!* Then Henry started heating up the second pot.

"We're going to need a really big bowl!" said Benny.

"No, something even bigger!" said Jessie. "Big like a bathtub!"

Uncle Flick brought in a very large plastic storage tub. "I just bought it to store holiday decorations," he said. "Though it's not quite as big as a bathtub."

"It's big enough to be *my* bathtub!" Benny said.

When the first batches of popcorn were finished, Henry dumped them into the tub.

"What are we going to put on it?" Violet asked. "Is there enough butter in the fridge?"

"No, and it's too messy anyway," said Jessie. "I have a better idea." She had gathered things from the pantry—Parmesan cheese, herbs, spices, salt. She poured a little of each into a plastic bag, then shook the bag. She sprinkled the mixture over the popcorn. Everyone tasted it.

"Delicious!" said Uncle Flick. The others agreed.

"Now all we have to do is make a lot more!" said Jessie.

Violet found an old coffee can and made holes in the plastic lid to make a

big shaker for the popcorn seasoning. While Joey and Henry worked at the stove popping popcorn, Violet shook seasoning mixture over the popcorn while Jessie scooped it into small paper bags. Then Grandfather and Benny loaded the golf cart with the bags and drove them to the theater. Uncle Flick lined them up on the counter of the snack bar to sell. He put up a sign that Violet made. It said:

No snack bar service tonight.
We are sorry!
But please enjoy fresh cheese popcorn!
Only 75 cents a bag.

By now the drive-in theater had opened for the evening. The customers who came to the snack bar were surprised to see the sign, but they were glad to have popcorn.

"It's delicious," said one woman. "And such a good price."

The children and Joey worked in the kitchen of the Fletcher house for another hour, popping as much popcorn as they could. When there was one last big batch in the tub, they took it over to the snack bar, where it would be ready to be scooped into bags. And Benny had found something even better than bags.

"Wow," he said, holding up two of the plastic buckets that said GET SPEEDY DEALS AT BRINKER'S AUTO on them. "These are perfect for popcorn!"

"You're right, Benny," said Jessie. She spotted Dan Brinker walking by the snack bar. She grabbed one of the buckets and ran after him. "Mr. Brinker! Do you have any more of these buckets that we can use for serving popcorn?"

"Sure," said Dan. "I've got plenty more! I'll dash across the street and bring them over in a jiffy!" He winked and hurried off.

"Thanks!" Jessie called. She turned around and went back inside the snack bar. She helped her sister and brothers serve popcorn while Joey rang up customers.

Uncle Flick grinned. "You really saved the day, kids," he said.

"We're glad we could help," said Violet.

"Maybe I can help, too," said a voice from the doorway of the snack bar. It was Mr. Duke. He was carrying a cooler and a bag of ice. "I . . . I heard what happened. And I brought over some soda from my stand."

Uncle Flick scratched his head. "Why, thank you, Duke. But you know, I'm letting folks bring in food from your place tonight. You didn't have to do this."

"I know," Mr. Duke said. "But I'm sorry about last night, too. I lost my temper. And I know that you didn't break my sign." He lugged the cooler and ice to the snack bar counter.

"Yes," said Uncle Flick. "Whoever's playing tricks around here is playing them on both of us."

As the Aldens scooped bags of popcorn, Mr. Duke and Uncle Flick opened sodas and filled cups with ice. The children listened as the two men talked for the first time in a long time.

"Is it true you might sell the theater, Flick?" Mr. Duke asked, as he got ready to leave.

"Yes it is," Uncle Flick replied. "But I'm going to make sure it doesn't close down."

"That's good to hear," said Mr. Duke. "Because I can't imagine life without the Diamond Drive-In. I don't know what would happen to my hot dog stand if the theater wasn't around." He chuckled. "Though it's not going to be as much fun without you around to argue with."

Uncle Flick laughed, too.

Henry whispered to Jessie, "We're not any closer to solving the mystery," he said. "But at least we've helped fix a friendship."

CHAPTER 6

What Everyone Wants

A half hour later, the popcorn the Aldens made was still selling well. So well, in fact, that they were running out of containers to serve it in. Violet looked at the crowd in the snack bar and began to worry.

"Shouldn't Dan Brinker be here by now, Jessie? You said he was bringing more buckets for us to use," she said.

Jessie looked at her watch. "I guess something came up at his store," she said. "I'll go to Duke's Dogs and see if I can get some spare

70

bags." She was sure that Mr. Duke would be helpful, now that he and Uncle Flick were friendly again. She hurried out the door and ran across the lot.

Not too long after she left, Uncle Flick turned to the other children. "Why don't you get a soda, kids? Joey and I can take it from here. You've done plenty."

Henry, Violet, and Benny were glad to have a break. They walked out to the theater lot with their sodas. There was a small playground at the front of the theater near the screen, and they sat on the swings and watched the sun set.

"Why does everyone have to wait until dark to watch the movie?" Benny asked. "At home we don't need to turn out the lights to watch TV."

"Watching a movie in a theater isn't the same as TV," Henry explained. "The projector throws flickering light on a screen. The darkness makes this easier to see. But if the sun was out—or if the lights were on—it would be much harder to see the movie."

Violet was thinking about this. "That's sort of like the ghost!" she said. "Remember how we couldn't see it when Uncle Flick turned on the lights out here in the theater?"

"You're right," said Henry. "Maybe this ghost is just . . . made of light somehow. We'll have to get closer next time we see it."

"And we won't turn on the lights and scare it away!" said Benny.

Meanwhile, Jessie was at Duke's Dogs, hoping Mr. Duke had some spare bags that they could use for popcorn.

"Of course I've got extra bags," Mr. Duke told her. "Let me get them."

Jessie looked around the hot dog stand while she waited. There were plenty of customers eating at picnic tables. One of them looked familiar. It was Dan Brinker. He had three empty hot dog wrappers and a half-eaten tray of fries in front of him. He was reading a magazine. It looked like he'd been sitting and eating for a long time. Why hadn't he brought over the buckets like he'd said he would?

Maybe he forgot, Jessie thought. *Or maybe he made a mistake and didn't have any after all.* She wondered if she should ask him. But then Dan had started to talk to a young woman in a Duke's Dogs uniform. He laughed and joked with her as she picked up the wrappers from his table. Just then, Mr. Duke brought out a bundle of paper bags for Jessie.

"Thank you, Mr. Duke," she told him.

As she hurried out she overheard just a little bit of Dan Brinker's conversation with the young woman. "If you ask me," he was saying, "I think that Flick is up to no good."

* * *

After all the popcorn-making, the Alden children were tired. They went back to the Fletcher house. Grandfather brought them sandwiches on the porch, and they sat on the steps with Watch. They all ate and looked out over the theater filled with cars. Tonight, the first movie was *Pirate Spy*. They could see it on the giant screen in the distance.

"It almost doesn't matter that we can't hear

the movie from here," Henry said. "We've seen it twice already!"

"And we know the story," said Violet. "I wish we could say the same for this mystery. So many things are happening! I'm sure it all fits together somehow—but how?"

Jessie nodded. "I know what you mean. It's like when we watched this movie for the first time," she said, pointing towards the screen. "We didn't know why the pirate captain was acting so strangely. We didn't know it was because he wanted to steal the diamond ring for himself."

"But then, the second time we saw the movie, we knew he never took off his boots for a *reason*," said Henry. "He'd hidden the ring there! It made sense once we knew what he wanted."

Jessie had an idea just then. She took out her notebook and opened it to a new page.

"What does everyone want?" she asked. "Everyone involved in this mystery, that is. Maybe if we thought about that, it would help."

"I think you're right, Jessie," said Henry.

So Jessie wrote WHAT EVERYONE WANTS at the top of the page.

"Let's start with Amy," she said.

"She seems worried about the theater. She wants . . . to keep her job, I guess," said Violet. "And she wants us to stay away from that shed."

Benny wanted very much to say something about the shed. Should he? he wondered. But he took another big bite of sandwich instead.

"What about Joey?" asked Violet.

"I think Joey wants to help Uncle Flick," Henry said. "Even if Uncle Flick doesn't think so."

Jessie wrote that down, too. She bit her pencil as she thought. "What if Joey wants to make trouble for Mr. Duke? Maybe he thinks that would help Uncle Flick," she said.

"I guess that's possible," said Henry. "But we don't know for sure. So write it down with a question mark."

So Jessie did. Next she wrote DAN BRINKER on the page. "What does *he* want?"

"To sell cars!" Benny said. "And put ads up all over town!"

Violet giggled. "He wants 'speedy deals!'" she said.

"And he wants to run the theater, too," Henry added.

Jessie wrote it all down. Soon she had a list:

WHAT EVERYONE WANTS

AMY— Wants to keep her job.

Wants us to stay away from shed.

JOEY—Wants to help Uncle Flick.

Wants to make trouble for Mr. Duke???

DAN BRINKER—Wants to sell cars.

Wants "speedy deals."

Wants to put ads all over town.

Wants to run the theater.

MR. DUKE: Wants to stay in business.

Wants theater to stay open, too.

UNCLE FLICK: Wants to sell the theater.

"Dan Brinker wants to do lots of things," Violet said, looking at the list.

"Dan Brinker *says* lots of things, too," Jessie said. She told her sister and brothers what she'd overheard at Duke's Dogs. "He said he thought Uncle Flick was up to no good."

"Wait a minute," said Henry. "He told us the same thing about Mr. Duke last night, remember? So whose side is he on?"

"I would think he'd have to be on *both* their sides," said Violet. "He wants to buy the theater from Uncle Flick. And he needs to get along with Mr. Duke next door."

"Well, maybe he didn't really mean what he said," Jessie said. "Maybe he says things that he thinks other people *want* to hear. He seems very good at that."

"But he's not good at watching movies!" Benny said suddenly. The other children turned and looked at him. What on Earth did he mean?

Benny pointed to the movie screen. It showed the scene in *Pirate Spy* when the captain found the buried treasure chest. The captain grinned as he dug it out of the sand.

"Remember when I told Dan Brinker that this was my favorite scene?" Benny asked. "Then he said he liked it too. He said he liked when the captain opened up the chest and found the gold! But that's not what really happened in the movie. Look!"

The children watched the movie as the captain opened the treasure chest. His smile vanished. The chest was empty!

"That's right!" Henry exclaimed. "We all thought there would be gold in the chest—but there wasn't! Dan must have forgotten about that part of the movie."

"But it's a really important part of the movie," said Jessie. "It changes the whole story. And Dan Brinker has seen the movie more than once—just like us!"

"Maybe he didn't really watch it closely," said Violet. "Maybe he was busy doing something else."

Jessie wrote that down in her notebook, too. Then she looked at the list again. "Now we know what everyone wants, but we still don't know what's going on! Or what this has to do with the ghost!"

"Maybe it'll all make sense later," said Henry. "And as for the ghost, I think we should go look for it tonight."

CHAPTER 7

To Catch a Ghost

It was late when the second movie ended and the last of the cars had left the drive-in theater. Uncle Flick had returned to the house, and all seemed quiet outside.

Watch stood at the door to the porch. He wanted to go for one last walk before bedtime.

"We'll take him," Jessie told Grandfather. The children put on their shoes and found their flashlights. Jessie picked up Watch's leash. Then they walked across the lawn of the Fletcher house toward the theater. Everything was dark—except for the neon sign that read DUKE'S DOGS. It shone brightly in the distance.

"Look, Mr. Duke's sign is fixed!" said Violet. "We were so busy tonight we didn't even notice."

The children and Watch walked towards the sign to get a closer look. When they had gotten as close as they could, they were behind the movie screen. They were close enough to the road to hear cars going by. Though it was night, the Aldens didn't need their flashlights, because the pink and orange glow of the big neon sign was so bright. It lit up the back of the screen.

"Wow," said Jessie. "The other day I thought that someone was hiding something back here. But it's too bright to hide anything! You can see almost everything from the road."

"But wait," Violet said. "What if that's why the sign was broken last night?"

Henry thought about this. "That's possible.

All along we've thought someone broke the sign to make Mr. Duke angry. But maybe somebody wanted it to be dark back here."

"But why?" Jessie said. "There's nothing here." She looked on the ground by the screen. Nothing.

Violet wasn't looking at the ground. She was looking up and she saw something along the top of the screen. *Had that always been there?* she wondered. It was high up and hard to see. She wanted to look closer. But then Benny made her forget what she was doing.

"Ghost!" he said, in a very loud whisper. *"Ghost!"* Watch started barking, too.

The children turned and saw the ghostly figure. It walked along a fence in the theater lot. The children hurried out to see it better. But while Jessie, Violet, and Benny raced towards the ghost, Henry did not. He turned and ran toward the projection booth.

"Hey!" he called. The others stopped and watched him as he ran up the steps of the booth and threw open the door.

"Henry, what are you doing?" Violet yelled.

Amy and Joey were in the booth. The film projector was on. Amy gasped and then reached over to turn it off. As soon as she did, the ghost disappeared.

"I knew it!" said Henry. The other children had run up to join him. "I knew the ghost had to be a movie of some kind."

Jessie glared at Amy and Joey. "Why were you doing that? Why were you trying to make the theater seem haunted?" she said.

"I know why!" Benny said. But he wasn't able to finish. Just then, Uncle Flick drove up in his golf cart with Grandfather.

"What's all this about?" he said to Amy and Joey. "I heard voices out here, and I saw this 'ghost' of yours. What are you two up to?" he was very angry.

"We can explain," said Joey.

"You'll do no such thing!" growled Uncle Flick. "I've had it! You're done here! You're—"

"Wait!" Benny yelled. He turned to Joey and Amy. "Tell him!" he said. "Tell Uncle Flick about the haunted house!"

"What?" said Jessie.

"How did you know?" said Amy.

"Haunted house?!" said Uncle Flick. "What are you talking about?"

"I'll show you!" said Benny. "Follow me!"

* * *

Benny led them all to the storage shed, where Amy had told the children not to go. Benny pulled open the door.

"Turn on the light!" he said to Joey.

Joey did. And the children couldn't believe what was inside.

"Yikes! A huge spider!" Violet said. Then she laughed.

"Oh my gosh, look at that bat!" Jessie exclaimed. And she laughed, too.

"Wow, that mummy is amazing!" said Benny.

The shed was filled with all kinds of haunted house things—fake skeletons, cobwebs, and plastic bats hanging from the ceiling. There were spooky gravestones made from painted wood, and even a casket with a lid that lifted

to show a mummy inside.

"This stuff is even better than the haunted house they have every year at the Greenfield Town Hall!" Henry said.

Amy grinned. "We've been working on it for two months," she said.

"It's very impressive," said Grandfather. "But what's it all for? And why were you keeping it secret?"

Joey pushed the hair out of his eyes. He turned to Uncle Flick. "Well, see, Amy and I had this idea to do a special event here at the theater this fall. We would call it 'Haunted House Days' and open the theater during the day."

"And at night we would show monster movies. And have hayrides," said Amy.

"And we'd decorate the whole theater with all this spooky stuff and special effects. But . . ." said Joey.

"Go on," said Uncle Flick.

"We were afraid that you wouldn't want to do it. We were worried you'd think it was too much work. So we decided to do it all by ourselves and surprise you," Joey said.

"During the day, we worked on making things here in the shed," said Amy. "And at night, we tested out the 'ghost' special effect. I'm a film student at college, so I made a short movie of Joey walking around draped in a sheet. Then we projected it against the fence so that it looked like a ghost."

"It really *did* look like one," Jessie said. The other children agreed.

"But we never meant to scare anyone for real," said Amy. "We're so sorry about that."

Joey looked down at his feet. "And we're sorry we haven't been keeping a better eye on things. If I hadn't been here painting stuff maybe the snack bar wouldn't have been vandalized."

"It's not your fault, Joey," said Uncle Flick. He didn't look angry now. He had a wistful smile. "I just wished you'd told me about your ideas. All along I thought you weren't interested in helping run the Diamond Drive-In. I wish I'd known before I decided to sell it." He sighed. "But this 'Haunted House Days' is a fine idea. It'll be a good thing to do at the end of the season. It'll be a great way to say good-bye to the theater."

Joey and Amy looked at each other, and then at the Aldens. They were wistful, too.

"Yes," said Joey. "It will."

CHAPTER 8

Speedy Deals

It was Monday morning, the last full day of the Aldens' visit. Tomorrow morning they would return to Greenfield. Since the Diamond Drive-In was closed on Mondays, they had the day all to themselves.

"I'm going over to Dan Brinker's auto store this morning," said Grandfather at breakfast. "Would you kids like to come along?"

"Are we going to get a new car?" Benny asked.

"No, not this year," Grandfather said. "But

sometimes it's fun to look at the latest models."

"Good idea," said Jessie. The other children nodded.

So they all went across the road to the car dealership. It was in a big glass building surrounded by rows and rows of shiny cars. It seemed more like a circus than a store. There were balloons everywhere, and bright painted signs that said *Great Deals!* All the salespeople wore red jackets. There was a huge showroom with cars on display. The Aldens liked getting into each one and smelling the new car smell.

Dan Brinker seemed very glad to see them. "So! Are you looking for a family car? I love families!"

"Oh, we can't buy anything right now," Grandfather said. "We're happy with the car we have now. But I just like to see the new models! Please don't mind us—we're just looking."

"Ah, yes, it's good to plan ahead," said Dan. He was very friendly. But he also followed Grandfather all around the showroom.

"This is the hottest style around," he told Grandfather, pointing to a bright yellow car. "We've got two left. I'll give you a special low price so you can drive it home today!"

Grandfather shook his head. "As I said before, I'm not interested in buying today. Or even this year."

"I know you don't *need* a car now," Dan replied. "But you might need one next year. And if you get it now, you'll be planning ahead!"

"No, thank you," Grandfather said firmly.

Dan turned to the children. "I bet you kids want a new car, don't you?"

"No, that's okay," said Jessie. "But speaking of buying, is it true you're going to buy the Diamond Drive-In Theater?"

"Yes, indeed!" said the car salesman. "I love the Diamond!"

"So you're going to keep the place open as a drive-in theater?" Henry asked.

Dan smiled. "I promised Flick Fletcher that the screen would always stay standing," he said.

The children wanted to ask Dan Brinker more questions. But one of his employees walked up and handed him a cordless phone.

"It's the bank," the man said.

"Sorry, kids," Dan told the Aldens. "I've been waiting for this important call." He leaned against one of the cars and started to talk on the phone.

Grandfather wanted to look at some of the new cars in the lot outside, so the Aldens walked towards the door. As they were leaving, Dan started to shout into the phone.

"What do you mean he wants a little more time? I want to buy it now! No ... I've planned ahead for this deal! I want it to be speedy!" He sounded upset. The children didn't hear the rest, though. It would have been rude to listen in. But they couldn't help but wonder if he was talking about the Diamond Drive-In Theater.

"Why is he in such a hurry?" Jessie wondered.

"Maybe he just likes to do everything fast,"

Violet said. "He sure talks fast."

As the Aldens got back into the minivan, a saleswoman in a red jacket waved good-bye.

"Come back to Brinker's Auto Store soon!" she said. "We're the biggest place in town to buy a car. And we're getting even bigger!"

* * *

They had just finished lunch at Uncle Flick's house when there was an urgent knock on the door. It was Mr. Duke.

"Flick! I heard a rumor that you're selling the theater to Dan Brinker!" he said as he marched into the kitchen where the Aldens were clearing the table.

"Yes, we're discussing it," said Uncle Flick.

Mr. Duke shook his head. "Are you crazy? Are you sure he's not planning to shut it down and turn it into another sales lot? He's just across the street! How do you know he's going to keep it open?"

"Well, because he said so," Uncle Flick

replied. "He knows I wouldn't sell it to him unless he swore that the movie screen would stay standing. And that's just what he promised."

Mr. Duke scratched his head. "I don't know," he said. "I just don't quite trust him. Maybe you should think about this."

"I'm not going to rush into this, if that's what you're worried about." He patted Mr. Duke on the back.

"That's good to know," said Mr. Duke. "Because if you change your mind about selling the theater to Dan Brinker, you can always sell it to me."

Uncle Flick's eyes narrowed. "What do you mean, Duke?" His voice sounded cold.

Mr. Duke tried to explain. "Nothing! I . . . I mean . . . I wish you weren't selling the theater in the first place. But if you need someone trustworthy to buy it, someone who will keep it going . . . *I* could buy it. That's all I'm saying." He stepped back. The children could see he hadn't meant to make Uncle Flick angry.

"Oh, is *that* what you want?" said Uncle Flick. "To take this place over? Is that why you've been playing all those pranks? You've been trying to drive me to sell the place, haven't you?!"

Now it was Mr. Duke's turn to get angry. "Now, Flick, you *know* that wasn't me. I would never do that! We've been working next door to each other for thirty years! We haven't always gotten along, but how dare you think I'd play tricks!" Mr. Duke turned around and walked out of the kitchen. A moment later everyone heard the door slam.

Uncle Flick's face was red. He took a deep breath. "I'm sorry. I guess we lost our tempers."

Grandfather put his hand on his old friend's shoulder. "Flick, do you want to go for a walk?"

"We can finish cleaning up here," Jessie offered.

Finally Uncle Flick managed a smile. "Thanks, folks. Yes, perhaps I need to take a walk. And think." He left the room with

Grandfather. After a moment the children saw them walking down the road towards the drive-in.

"We may have solved the mystery of the ghost at the drive-in," Henry said, "but we still haven't figured out who's behind the pranks."

The oldest Alden was right. They still hadn't found out who had switched the movie sound the other night, or broken the Duke's Dogs sign, or vandalized the snack bar.

"Someone's trying to ruin everything," Benny said.

"We'll just have to stop that someone," Jessie replied.

CHAPTER 9

The Truth Unfolds

Henry, Jessie, Violet, and Benny sat around the kitchen table. Jessie had her notebook open to a new page. On it was a list of names she'd written:

AMY
JOEY
DAN BRINKER
MR. DUKE

One of these people, the children were sure, had been causing the trouble at the Diamond Drive-In Theater.

Violet pointed to Amy's and Joey's names. "I don't think they did it. I think they want to save the theater."

Everyone else agreed. So Jessie crossed Amy and Joey off the list.

"What about that argument we heard to-day?" Henry asked. "Do you think that Mr. Duke is really trying to force Uncle Flick to sell him the theater?"

"No," Jessie said. She tapped her pen, because she was thinking hard.

"I don't think so, either," said Violet. Benny nodded, too.

Jessie kept tapping her pen. "But . . . but what if Dan Brinker is? What if *he's* the one who's doing all the pranks?"

Henry shook his head. "That doesn't make sense, Jessie. Uncle Flick already likes Dan and *wants* to sell the theater to him. Dan doesn't have to make him do anything."

"That's true," said Jessie. "But there's something about Dan Brinker that I don't trust. For one thing, he said he would help us with the popcorn last night. He said he had extra buckets. But then he never brought them!"

"Perhaps he just didn't have any extras after all," Violet said. "Who's to say he didn't want to help us?" She always tried to think the best about people.

Henry looked thoughtful. "Well, if you think about it, whoever wrecked the snack bar certainly wouldn't want to help us."

"Do you think that 'whoever' was Dan?" Jessie asked.

"Who knows? There's no way we can prove it," Henry said. "All we can do is think of reasons why he'd play pranks."

"Maybe he just wanted Uncle Flick to sell him the theater faster!" Benny said. "He likes speedy deals! Remember we wrote it down?"

"Very good, Benny," Jessie said. Then she flipped back in her notebook to the WHAT EVERYONE WANTS page. "Here's another note I wrote down other night: 'Dan Brinker says things that other people like to hear.' "

"Gosh," said Violet. "Is that the same thing as lying?"

"Not always," said Jessie. "But sometimes, yes it is."

Suddenly Henry leapt up, the way he always did when he had a big idea. He snapped his fingers. "That's it! I think Dan is lying to Uncle Flick!"

"Lying about what?" Violet asked.

"Lying about keeping the drive-in theater open!" said Jessie. Her eyes got wide. "Yes, it makes perfect sense."

Henry went on. "Dan has been telling Uncle Flick he'll keep running the theater, but really, he doesn't. Because—"

Benny finished for him. "Because he wants to tear it down and make his car store bigger! Just like the lady there said today. Remember?"

Violet repeated the words. " 'We're the biggest place in town to buy a car. And we're getting even bigger.' Oh, no."

The children didn't say anything for a moment. And then Jessie sighed a heavy sigh.

"Maybe we're right about Dan Brinker, but we won't know for sure until it's too late. Because we don't have any proof," she said.

"Why don't we just tell Uncle Flick that we don't trust Dan?" Henry suggested.

Jessie threw up her hands. "Mr. Duke just tried to do the same thing. And look what happened! Uncle Flick got angry." She paced around the kitchen. "If only we could catch him doing something . . . making trouble at the theater. But I don't think we will."

The others knew what Jessie meant. The theater was closed that day, and all the other pranks had happened on days it was open. There didn't seem to be anything they could do. They all slumped in their chairs. Benny fidgeted and played with a scrap of broken balloon he'd found in his pocket. He stretched it and snapped it with his fingers.

"Benny, where'd you find that?" Jessie asked.

"Behind the screen the other day," said Benny as he stretched and snapped some more.

"That looks like it came off of one of Dan

Brinker's cars," Henry pointed out. "It's white, like some of the balloons on his car that very first night. The night he saw the ghost."

"And we figured out there had been a car parked behind the screen," said Jessie. "He must have driven it back there. But why?"

Violet was remembering the thing she'd seen behind the screen the night before. She had forgotten about it until now, and she wondered if it was important. She glanced at Jessie's notebook and at the list they'd made. *Dan Brinker—Wants to sell cars . . . wants to put ads all over town.* She remembered hearing him on the phone. *I've planned ahead for this deal,* he said. What did that mean?

"You guys?" she said. "We have to go look at something right now."

* * *

A few minutes later the four children were standing behind the movie screen.

"Jessie, remember that strange bundle you said you saw back here the other day?" Violet asked her sister.

"Yes, but I told you, it's gone now," said Jessie.

Violet pointed upwards. "Is that it up there?" she asked.

Jessie looked up, and there, way up along the top of the screen, was something that looked like a very big soft rolled-up blind. It was up so high that it was hard to notice, and since it was in back of the screen, it couldn't be seen from the theater lot.

"Oh, my gosh, I think it is!" Jessie said. "It's the same color and everything."

Uncle Flick and Grandfather heard the children's voices while they were on their walk. They came behind the screen and joined them. Soon Uncle Flick was peering up at the strange rolled-up thing.

"What on Earth is that? I didn't put that up there!" he said.

"Look, there are cords attached to it," Henry pointed out. "They're tied to the ladders on either side. They must keep it from unrolling."

"Well, why don't we unroll it then, and see

what it is?" said Uncle Flick. "Where's Joey? He can help us."

Before long, Henry and Joey were carefully climbing the two metal ladders that ran down the back of the screen. Henry held on tight while he worked to untie the cord and grab it. Joey did the same. Finally they were both holding the cords taut. The rolled-up thing wavered in the wind a little bit, and they could see it was some kind of nylon fabric, the kind used to make parachutes or flags. What was it?

"On the count of three, we'll let go of the cords," shouted Joey. "One, two—three!"

They let go, and the fabric unrolled.

It was an enormous banner, almost as large as the screen! There were words on it:

THE DIAMOND DRIVE-IN IS CLOSED.

COMING SOON—

BRINKER'S AUTO STORE'S EAST LOT!

BIGGER AND BETTER! DRIVE OUT

WITH A DIAMOND DEAL!

The banner had turned the back of the movie screen into a giant billboard that faced the road.

Everyone stared at it in surprise.

"*Closed?* Is that what Dan means to do?" Uncle Flick shouted.

"He's got some nerve," said Grandfather. "To put up that banner even before the place was sold."

"Oh, my goodness," Violet said. "We were right. Dan Brinker really was lying about keeping the drive-in theater open."

Jessie nodded. "He promised the screen would stay standing. Only he wasn't telling the whole truth."

"He's in big trouble!" said Benny. "*That's* the whole truth now."

CHAPTER 10

The Diamond Is Forever

The giant banner on the movie screen could be seen from all around. Cars on the road slowed down to get a better look. A small crowd gathered in front of Duke's Dogs to stare at it. They all wondered about the sign—would the Diamond Drive-In Theater really close down?

"Wait! Stop!" someone called across the road. It was Dan Brinker. He had seen the banner unfurl, too. Now he was hurrying across the road to reach Uncle Flick and the

Aldens. "No, no, it's too early!" he shouted as he reached them. He panted as he tried to catch his breath. "No . . . nobody was supposed to see that yet!"

"Is that so, Dan?" Uncle Flick said. He glared at Dan. "Just what were you trying to do?"

Dan's forehead was sweaty. He stammered, "I . . . I had that banner ready so I could display it as soon as the papers were signed! I wanted this theater closed the first chance I got!"

"You were trying to trick me, Dan!" Uncle Flick growled. "You knew I'd never sell this place to you if it meant closing down the theater, so you said you were going to keep it open! But you lied! You weren't even going to wait until the end of the season!"

"And you were the one who caused all the trouble around here!" Joey added bitterly. "Why? We trusted you!"

"I think I know one reason why," Jessie said to Dan. "You had to sneak around the theater to put that banner in place! You brought it over in your car on Thursday night. Then on Friday you broke Duke's sign so you could climb up the back of the screen!"

"And the ladder made your hands dirty," said Benny. "That's why you didn't take any of my popcorn on Friday night!"

Dan Brinker had lowered his head. "Yes," he said, "You figured it out. I did some of the pranks to create a distraction. And so Flick Fletcher would sell me the place faster."

"You were also trying to make Uncle Flick and Mr. Duke mad at each other, weren't you?" Violet asked.

Dan hung his head even lower. "Yes. That, too. I'm sorry."

Uncle Flick folded his arms. "Dan, you'll have to pay for the damages to the snack bar kitchen. You've done things that are against the law, so I'm going to have to call the police. And, just to be clear, the deal is off!"

"I know," said Dan. "What I did was wrong. All along I knew, deep down, that it was wrong. I should have stopped when I saw the ghost the other night."

"What do you mean?" Jessie asked.

"I know the ghost wasn't real," Dan said. "But I'll tell you, I was so scared when I saw it! I thought it was some kind of message, telling me I had to stop cheating people, that I had to slow down." He looked thoughtful. "I wish I had."

"Maybe you will now," said Henry. The others nodded in agreement.

Dan Brinker wiped the sweat from his forehead and stood up straight. He walked over to the giant banner. He yanked on one of the corners until the banner came loose and crumpled to the ground. Then he turned and walked back across the road to his store, with his head down.

* * *

"I'm glad you're not selling the drive-in after all, Flick," said Mr. Duke the next evening. He and Uncle Flick were sitting in lawn chairs in front of the Diamond Drive-In screen. The mini-van was parked nearby. The children and

Grandfather had decided to stay one more night to see the new movies, *Space Dogs* and *The Rainforest Giant*. Now they were all having a picnic before the movie started. Mr. Duke had bought over food from his stand.

"I'll bet you're glad, Duke," said Uncle Flick. "Especially since I've decided to let my customers bring in your hot dogs."

"They're really good hot dogs," said Jessie as she sat down in a nearby lawn chair. The other Aldens joined her, and soon they were all enjoying the food together.

"I love the onion rings!" said Benny as he picked up a big one and took a bite.

"And don't forget the popcorn from the snack bar," said Violet. "That's good, too."

"Yes, indeed," said Uncle Flick. "We've gotten a new popcorn machine, but we're also going to keep a big shaker of Jessie's popcorn topping on the counter. That is, if you'll give me the recipe."

"Of course!" said Jessie, who smiled proudly.

"I bet Joey and Amy will be happy to be part of the business," Henry said to Uncle Flick.

"I'm making Joey a manager, and Amy will be in charge of special events," Uncle Flick replied. "And now they're planning all kinds of interesting things. In fact, they just borrowed the slide projector. I wonder what they'll use it for."

After a beautiful sunset in the distance behind the screen, it was almost time for the movie to begin. The Aldens took their seats in the minivan. Watch curled up on Jessie's lap. Grandfather turned on the car stereo.

"Here we go," said Henry, as the screen lit up. Then an announcement appeared on the screen:

COMING SOON!

FALL FESTIVAL

AT THE DIAMOND DRIVE-IN THEATER!

HAUNTED HOUSE GALORE!

MOVIES, MYSTERIES, AND MORE!

"Hooray!" Benny shouted as the other children applauded.

"Can we come back next month and go to this, Grandfather?" Violet asked.

"Of course," Grandfather said. "We wouldn't miss it for the world."

"Look!" said Jessie. "There's another announcement!" She pointed to the screen. Now it read:

WE WOULD LIKE TO THANK THE ALDENS—
HENRY, JESSIE, VIOLET, BENNY, AND THEIR
GRANDFATHER—FOR SAVING OUR THEATER.
HONK IF YOU LOVE
THE BOXCAR CHILDREN!

Beep! Bee-beep! Beep! went all the cars in the theater lot. *Beep-beep! Beep!*

"Oh, my goodness!" Violet giggled.

"It sounds like a traffic jam," Henry said, laughing.

"But even better!" said Benny. "Because we can beep back!" Then he reached over and pressed the horn on the minivan. *Beep! Beep! Beep!*

GERTRUDE CHANDLER WARNER discovered when she was teaching that many readers who like an exciting story could find no books that were both easy and fun to read. She decided to try to meet this need, and her first book, *The Boxcar Children*, quickly proved she had succeeded.

Miss Warner drew on her own experiences to write the mystery. As a child she spent hours watching trains go by on the tracks opposite her family home. She often dreamed about what it would be like to set up housekeeping in a caboose or freight car — the situation the Alden children find themselves in.

While the mystery element is central to each of Miss Warner's books, she never thought of them as strictly juvenile mysteries. She liked to stress the Aldens' independence and resourcefulness and their solid New England devotion to using up and making do. The Aldens go about most of their adventures with as little adult supervision as possible — something else that delights young readers.

Miss Warner lived in Putnam, Connecticut, until her death in 1979. During her lifetime, she received hundreds of letters from girls and boys telling her how much they liked her books.